MW00681609

EAGLE EYES

THE DESCENDANTS OF WHITE WOLF

A SHORT STORY BY

TAMMY LASH

EAGLE EYES

Copyright © 2018 by Tammy Lash
Cover Design: by Tammy Lash
Interior Design by: Savannah Jezowski at Dragonpenpress.com
Photography by: Tammy Lash and Kelsey Lash at Kelsey Lyn Photography

This book is the work of fiction. All incidents and dialogue, and all characters with the exception of certain well known historical and public places and figures, are the products of the author's imagination and are not to be construed as real. In all other respects, any resemblance to any persons alive or dead is purely coincidental.

ISBN: 978-0-692-04369-1

All Rights Reserved. This book may not be copied, reproduced, transmitted or stored by any means, including graphic, electronic or mechanical without the written consent of the author, except in cases of brief quotations in critical articles, news articles and reviews.

Printed and Published in the United States of America

WHITE WOLF
PUBLISHING

TABLE OF CONTENTS

DEDICATION

"I wonder if joy can't be subtle and sweet most days. Like the taste of Mom's chocolate pie."

- *Jeremy Gudwyne*

To Teri, Uncle Ron, and Mama.
Thank you for blessing me with your brave example in adversity. May you never lose sight of His blessings.

To our new hometown of Munising
where inspiration is as abundant as the waters of the
Gitchi-gami.

To our new friends in Munising who gave life to the characters.

Ojibwe
Words and Definitions

Gagiibiingwe Apakwaanaajiinh - Blind Bat

Giiwwanaadizi - Crazy

Gitchi-gami (Gitchee Gumee, Kitchi-gummi, Kitchi-gami) - The shining blue sea water, Big Sea, Huge Water, Great Water. Refers to Lake Superior

Makade-waagosh - Black Fox

Migizi - Eagle

Needonnisug - Brother

Niimi Biis Nigig - Dancing Otter

Ozhichige - He /she makes, builds, forms things

Waabishkaa Ma'iingan - White Wolf

EAGLE EYES

The sound came from the sky.

I pat a handful of sand onto the top of my mountain. The grains don't stick, and they avalanche down into the side of my shoe. I scoop the sides up and press the gritty mound down with a bounce. I don't usually make castles when I come out to the beach. Sixteen is a little too old to be playing around in the sand, after all.

"Don't look up. Don't look up. Don't—look—up." The waves speak over my words, and the wind snatches them away. I'm grateful for the deafening work of the wind and the waves. They help me feel less stupid for talking to myself.

"Thanks, Jay. Thanks a lot!" I shout the words meant for my absent brother and send them out toward the rolling *Gitchi-gami*. *Gitchi-gami* is the Ojibwe word for Lake Superior. It means *big sea*. Its mighty waves crash over the noise that took all my air to make.

The wind teases the hair under my hat and tickles underneath my nose. I need to take it in—to take a breath—but I don't want to. I want my body to feel as empty as I do. I count through the burn, and my ears soak in the conversation of the waves. At eight, the weight becomes too much to bear.

Nine, ten, eleven, twelve—I fill my nostrils with lake air and close my eyes as my chest rises.

Thirteen, fourteen, fifteen, sixteen—I blow the new air back out and let my shoulders fall.

Mom taught me how to do this—how to count through my breathing. It's supposed to calm me down. Most days, it works and takes away the tight feeling in my throat. The cold air is helping. It tastes good to my insides.

I drag my fingers around my mound to make a moat. I might fill it up if Jay doesn't get here soon, but I hope he does. I don't know how much longer I can keep the tight feeling away. It's the warning sign I get when I'm about to cry. Dad always tells me that a great man is a sensitive one, so I've never had a problem crying alone in my room or in the shower. The problem is, I don't want to do anything else these days once I start.

Wa-wa-wa-wa.

I pump down with both hands onto the top of my mountain to keep myself from looking up at my eagle. He's here—just like I thought he would be. He thinks I'm here to see him. That's exactly what I knew he would think.

"Funny. Really funny. *See* him? Go away, you crazy, crazy, bird. I'm not here for you—I'm here for Jay."

Giiwanaadizi. I chuckle into the wind. My eagle isn't the crazy one: I am. *I'm giiwanaadizi.* I'm giving the sand CPR. I wish I had brought my water bottle. My throat feels awful.

Inhale—one, two, three, four.

Exhale—five, six, seven, eight.

I can't lose it. Jay could show up at any moment. Crying makes him uncomfortable. His ticks go wild when he's uncomfortable. I can't—I *won't*—do that to him. My *needonnisug* has enough discomfort to handle without me adding to it.

I wish I were at home in my room. That's where I usually go to flip out, but today is Saturday. Everyone will be there. I wish I was soaking in the shower. That's the second-best place to go when my parents and Jay are home.

Super-hot water turns my face tomato red. I can walk out of the bathroom with my messed-up face and get zero hovering. When I come out all snotty and blotchy from my bedroom, I get a reaction from mom that makes me feel all jumbled and weird inside. Dad won't do anything; he'll just stay busy doing whatever it is that he's doing. Jay—he'll count and twist his shirt buttons until one of them pulls off, but Mom? Mom will rush over to me like I came in all skinned up after a fall from my mountain bike. She'll look nervous and scared, but then she'll use her super-polite, phone voice to ask if I'm okay.

It's the same exact six words—every time—in this pinched, boa-constricted tone.

"Jeremy, sweetheart—are you all right?"

It doesn't even sound like her. It's the tone she uses with strangers or with people who make her uncomfortable. Fear dipped in white chocolate—that's what her voice sounds like to me. I know fear. We've been the best of friends since I got the news, and I know white chocolate too. It's gross and disgustingly sweet.

I hate it when Mom asks if I'm okay. It's bait to get me to talk. I don't like talking, so I usually end up listening. To avoid a long, drawn-out, one-sided conversation, I'll pull a super-dorky smile and lie and say I'm fine, and then I'll get this sad weight in my chest when I walk away from her. I'll feel like it's all my fault that *she's* sad, and then I'll feel mad that God chose me to be this way. Why me? What did I do that was so bad to be punished like this? Isn't He supposed to love us and want the best for us? How is *this* loving me? How is *this* the best for me?

Wa-wa-wa-wa.

Migizi is stubborn. He wants to talk—but I don't want to. He should know better than anyone else that I'm stubborn, too. I won't look up. I won't look up. I won't—look—up. No matter how much he begs me to. I squint down at the sand and try to make out the shape I've made. It feels unnatural not looking up toward my eagle. I miss him, and this beach is reminding me of just how much I do. I slap my hands across my jeans. I can't see the sand bits, but I can feel that they're there. Sand sticks to everything— just like sadness does. I'll be wearing this stuff for days. I think I'll be sad probably forever.

I'm lucky I have the shower to melt down in. We haven't always been the proud owners of the greatest water heater ever

3

made. At one time, we had to time our showers. Dad told us that our old water heater in the closet hallway was too small for our super-clean family of four. He put Mom's oven timer in the bathroom to help us keep them short, so everyone could have a chance at hot water. Jay and I made a game out of it. I used to have the best time at one minute and thirty-two seconds, but that was before. After we got home from my appointment with a third eye doctor in April—the one that I now see every three months downstate—I had my worst time ever at ten minutes and fifty-six seconds. It could have been worse. The Lake Superior cold encouraged me out before I was ready. Being told you're going blind has its advantages. I didn't get into trouble with Dad. No tones, no speeches, no looks...nothing. He stopped at Menards the next day instead and got the biggest water heater in stock. He must have charged it. We can't afford big stuff like that. Now that Mom got her timer back in the kitchen, she doesn't burn her cookies anymore, and no one cares how long my showers are.

I wonder if Migizi is still soaring around? Just in case, I press a rock to the top of my sand blob to look busy and begin on a new blob. The rock represents the satellite dish I wish we had on top of our roof. We haven't had real TV since—forever. Traveling to U of M four times a year and getting fitted with special glasses each time with no insurance is expensive. Satellite TV was the first thing we had to let go. My friends asked me why I didn't use my unlimited data instead to watch movies from my phone. I don't have a cell phone anymore, either, and that alone stinks like a skunk in twenty-year-old socks. What kid doesn't have his own phone?? A kid with eyes that gobble up all his parents' money, that's who. But, really, does it matter? TV's, cell phones—I can't see either of them, so why do I even care?

"Migizi." I say his name into the wind like the magic word I feel it is and shake my head to organize the crazy thoughts bouncing around. I'm special. I'm weird. I'm broken. I could someday become one of the legends my Dad sings about at our

Pow Wows. No one knows about the "special" and "legend" part but me, Jay, and Migizi. How can I have a gift so awesome and a handicap so horrible all at the same time? The two play a tug-of-war with my emotions every single day.

I should have given Migizi a better name. It isn't at all creative like Native names should be, and if my Ojibwe-speaking grandpa were still alive, he would not be impressed. Maybe he would cut me some slack. I was only twelve when I named him. I had wanted to name him something cool in my native language, but I only knew a few baby words—small words that stuck out over the millions that grandpa had tried to teach me. Migizi was the best that I could do. It means eagle in Ojibwe.

I miss my eagle. I wonder if he misses me? I know he misses the fish I used to bring him. I should have grabbed some Whitefish from the freezer in the pole barn. Dad and Jay both have our fish quota for the winter already. They wouldn't have missed a filet or two—well, Jay would have. He's great at numbers. He would have noticed.

Inhale—one, two, three, four, five.

The air smells different here. You can smell sensations that inland smells usually drown out—the cold and the wet. The air is simpler too. It's one note. It's clean. The air smells clean at home, too, but living near the Hiawatha, the scent of the pines over takes everything.

Exhale—six, seven, eight, nine, ten.

I've missed the beach. I haven't had sand in my shoes since the waking of the birches in the spring. It's now fall and nearly time for them to go back to sleep.

Wa-wa-wa-wa.

"I'm not here for you, Migizi!" The lake rumbles over my shout, but I know my eagle heard me. I heard him.

Things haven't changed between us like I thought they would. It's been five months and I can still understand him. I keep my eyes down and hold my empty hands up to the sky. Maybe Migizi will go away when he discovers I don't have anything for him. I won't look up. I won't look up. I won't—look—up. No matter how much I want to.

I wish my brother hadn't picked this meeting spot. I shouldn't have agreed to come, but I did. My *needonnisug* always gets his way. Well, with me he does. Mom and Dad know how to say no. I haven't quite figured out how to. Mom says it's okay to be firm with Jay when it comes to what I want and what matters to me, but she said it in a way that made me feel she understands why I am the way I am toward my big brother. She also added that Jay and I aren't that different from all the other brothers on the planet. I think she's wrong. I don't know of any other big brothers that cry and throw fits when they hear *no* from their younger siblings. I still shouldn't have come. I should have told Jay *no*—but I hate it when my big brother cries. I don't like disappointing him. He gets enough of that from everyone else. I came because he seemed really excited about meeting me here. My *needonnisug* said he had something for me. Why couldn't he just give it me at home? Why didn't I just tell him *no*? Oh, yeah—that's right. It's because I *can't* say *no* and now I'm making sand castles on the Lake Superior beach I swore I would never come back to.

Disappointment.

I know how the word feels. That's why I won't look up to my eagle.

"Don't look up. Don't look up. Don't—look—up, Jer—don't you *dare*."

I'm such a weirdo. I used my own name, and I said it in rhyme, even. A wounded moan squeezes past the barricade in my throat. It wasn't the soothing chuckle of Dad's I was hoping it would be. I love my Dad's laugh, and when I hear it I feel warm and safe; my noise made me feel the exact opposite. What am I doing? Am I laughing? Crying? Can one do both at the same time? I'm talking to myself—and I find that to be hysterically funny—but the thought of not being able to see Migizi ever again makes me want to cry all messy and loud like my big brother. Using the word *weirdo* was a huge mistake. That's what they call my brother. When I hear them call him that, it hurts about as much as looking up to my eagle and never seeing him again.

My heart feels sloshy and heavy—like my shoes feel when the waves from the lake soak into them. There was a time when Migizi's call would make my heart beat super-fast, like how it used to beat after one of my three-mile runs. My eagle would help me feel lighter and happier about things. I don't feel my heart's beat anymore. Maybe it's because I haven't run since I've stopped wearing my glasses. Maybe it's because of my big brother and the realization I had last Christmas that he was born broken and would forever remain the same. Maybe it's because of my eyes. I was born broken, too, but things for me are different. I'm changing. I've been losing my sight a little bit every year since I was six.

The sand won't stay on my mountain no matter how hard I try. It's too dry. I guess I forgot you can't make a castle with dry sand. I lean forward and scratch my knuckles across a cluster of rocks warming in the sun and wait for a wave to come close. Is Migizi up there? Or did he give up and leave me? The need to see my friend again is too great. The lake rolls up to my fingertips. I look up.

I see bright.

I see blue.

I think I see smears of white.

I should be thankful. I can still see light, make out color, and see shapes—blurry, smeary shapes—but, I can still see something. According to my optimist dad, "it could be worse". Yeah, I guess things could be worse. Things could be pitch-black for me, but I'm not the glass-is-half-full kind of guy my dad is. I imagine my glass to be leaky, cracked, and just-a-few-drops-from-empty. Dark—blurry—it doesn't matter. Facts are facts. I'm legally blind, and I don't need working eyes to see that.

My dad? He's superman. He can do everything, and what he can't do he figures out. Maybe God should have let him be the blind one. He'd be handling this whole situation better than me. He wouldn't have to lock himself in the bathroom every night to keep things together during the day. He's a specimen of perfection. He's the man I wish I could someday grow up to be, but I know I can't. I'm not him. I'm me.

I can never be like Dad. Not now. Not ever, and especially not like this. Dad is the pride of the Ojibwe. He isn't the full-blooded Ojibwe that many of our friends are, but he's the oldest living relative of the legendary White Wolf and that makes him super important. In the summer, our family tours Pow Wows all over the state of Michigan to represent our people in the Upper Peninsula and to sing of the legend of my great-great-great grandparents. Dad sings about the White Wolf and the Ash Princess while I pound out the beat on my drum for my uncle. Uncle Jon is my dad's brother, and he's an award-winning dancer. He does this amazing dance to the song with his hoops. He normally uses ten, but he has used up to twenty. Uncle Jon magically transforms them into a giant sphere or a pair of eagle's wings all while stomping his feet to the rhythm of Dad's songs. Uncle Jon was supposed to teach me to dance, but I couldn't see the hoops well enough to make the simplest of his shapes—the eagle wings. He taught me to play the drum instead and that totally bummed me out. I really wanted to dance and learn to make the wings. I think Migizi would have liked that.

I sit back and shake the wet from my hand. I don't know if any of it made it to my sand mountain like I had wanted. I can't see enough detail to see where the drops fell. Pity is a strong current, and today I don't have enough strength to swim against it. Mom says joy is a choice and that it's up to me to find it "in all things." I don't think she realizes how super-hard that is to do. I mean, she's not the one who's as blind as a mole in sunglasses. I am. I hate having to make the conscious decision to choose joy every day.

Mom says it will get easier the more I do it. Lots of things get easier the more you do them—like solving an equation in Algebra or pounding in one of those ridiculously, teeny nails without whacking your fingers—but days like today make it hard to find the good in anything. I know I should listen to Mom—she's always right about these things—but today I don't feel like sifting. I feel like giving in. I want to lay back and let the tides of self-loathing pick me up and take me where it must.

I couldn't see Migizi. I knew I wouldn't. I think I'm going to puke. Maybe, if I try one more time I'll see him. I look up and shield my eyes. I scrunch my nose with my squint. I don't know why I flex my nose muscles like a nerd adjusting his glasses higher on his face. It's never helped me see any better. I squeeze my lids together super-tight and leave the teeniest of spaces to peer through. Usually, this *does* help...

...but not today.

Today, the sky is this bright, chilly blue that matches the temperature in the air. It looks icy and kind of yummy with the clouds smeared in—like the Blue Moon ice cream Jay and I would get at the café in town when we were younger. The café had a zillion different flavors to choose from, but the only kind we would ever get was Blue Moon. Jay got it because he doesn't like chunks of anything mixed in with his, and Blue Moon was just a flavor that he would always choose. Mom says it was the only kind that he would try in the times before me, even. I got it because I liked turning blue. My waffle cone would leak out of the bottom on our bike ride home, every time, no matter how fast I tried to eat it. My hands and forearms would be covered in sticky, blue streaks by the time we made it to the swing set in the backyard. I'd lick myself clean in our fort under the slide while Jay usually fiddled with whatever junk he had in his backpack. Watch parts, levers, gears, switches—Jay would click and clack things into place while I licked and lapped at my skin.

I miss our fort.

9

I miss watching Jay make things.

I miss turning blue.

Wa-wa-wa-wa.

I turn my head, so my ears can "see" where he's going. I fall back into the sand and smack the satellite dish off the top of my mountain when I lose "sight" of him. What on earth made me to think I could see Migizi? I can barely make out my castle. I'm surprised I could make out the stupid rock well enough to sail it across the beach.

Tappp. Tappp. Tappp. *Pic-Pic-Pic-Pic-Pic!*

This sound isn't Migizi—it's a hungry woodpecker in one of the trees. The rock satellite is digging into my palm: so much for chucking it across the beach. I sit up and throw it toward the direction of the lake. Woodpeckers are pretty—at least I remember them to be. There are eight different kinds of Woodpeckers in Michigan, and Grandpa and I have seen them all, back when binoculars still worked with my eyes. Most of them are feathered in the colors of fire—flame red and ash black, and they have these artistic areas of bleached white on their wings. Which one of the eight is complaining about his empty belly? If I were to guess, it would be a Hairy or a Downy, but I don't know which. I don't like not knowing anything for certain. I don't like having to rely on the pictures in my memory, either. Grandpa died just last winter and the only thing that I can visually recall about him are the old logging boots that he'd wear when he split wood—and that's because I have them in my room and am reminded of them every day. How long will pictures of the woodpeckers stay? The last time I saw one was when Grandpa and I went birding together before he died and left me. Grandpa's boots are a blur in the corner of my room. What happens when my eyes forget what those two blobs in the corner are supposed to be? My throat feels as narrow as a straw...

...what if I start crying and can't stop?

Jay isn't here yet. Maybe he forgot. I know I'll feel better if I let it out. I can pretend that I'm at home in the shower. I should—because maybe, just maybe, I'll see a little bit of Migizi this time. Sometimes for the briefest of moments I can see through the tears—kind of like how I used to see out of my glasses. It isn't hard to get them started. The pressure has been building behind my eyes since I got here.

The wind sets a challenge to my eyes when I scan the sky. Its icy breath burns. I need to blink, but I can't. I'm not going to until I find my eagle up there in the blue, but who am I to muscle against the wind? Who am I to think that I have any power against him? Lake Superior is at his mercy every day and he fails. How can *I* win the battle against his might? Who am *I* to think I can? I close my eyes. My "lenses" leak out and crawl in defeat down into my ears.

Who am I? I'm no one. I'm just Jeremy—the great-great-great grandson of the legendary *Waabishkaa Ma'iingan*—White Wolf, the hero who released my people from bondage. I'm just Jeremy, son of *Makade-waagosh*—Black Fox, my smart "can-figure-it-out-and-do-everything-and-anything" Dad. I'm just Jeremy, nephew to *Niimi Biis Nigig*—the Dancing Otter, who wins awards at every one of his dance competitions. I'm just Jeremy, brother to *Ozhichige*—Jay, the builder and maker of all things awesome. And then there's me. Plain old Jeremy, the blind kid that has yet to be given his Native name. Dad says I'll get it tonight at the bonfire, that he chose one months ago and the elders finally approved it. I bet I know what Dad chose. It's *Gagiibiingwe Apakwaanaajiinh*. Jeremy, the Blind Bat.

The sky blurs.

It does look cool this way. I reach up and ruffle my fingers underneath the color. I can feel the dance of the wind against my hand. I close it to capture its weight. I wish I could hold onto God's hand like I used to hold on to Dad's. Maybe things would be easier if He were here—like, *here*—like how Dad is. On our family hikes, when my eyes were just beginning to go crazy, Dad would lift me across all kinds of stuff—tree roots, hidden stumps, washed-out spots—the typical forest junk that would cause the "seeing" to stumble. I was never afraid on my hikes with Dad. I knew with him I'd be safe. I'd get to fly across anything that could hurt me. I wish God would do that with me. With my eyes—with my *needonnisug*—with this empty spot that I have with Grandpa being gone, with—with *everything*.

"They're putting in the new power lines today."

Jay startles me straight, and I lift the bottom of my shirt to dry the sides of my cheeks. My *needonnisug* shouts when he speaks and, honestly, his volume rubs my nerves raw at home most days; but here, with the noise of the lake, it sounds natural. Normal. He drops his tattered pack onto the sand. It's the pack he takes everywhere, even to church. I squint up to my brother and use my hand as a shield against the sun. He's the blob version of himself I've grown accustomed to, like a giant painted in soft, smeary watercolor. My watercolor brother has his hands on his hips and is looking out toward the water. He could easily be the model for the old black-and-white picture of the Ojibwe warrior on my dresser that I found in a free box at a garage sale.

"Hey, buddy. You made it. Good goin'—you remembered your jacket," I say. I sniff and wipe my nose on my sleeve. I can tell he's wearing his jacket. He looks puffier than usual. Deduction and educated guesses. Those are two of the techniques I use to hide what's happening to me. The wind is coming out of the north. Glassy eyes and runny noses are common side effects out here when it's blowing from that direction. Jay will be sniffing and wiping his own nose on his sleeve soon. He won't have a clue that I lost it.

Jay groans when he bends and plunks down in the sand next to me. My brother isn't an old guy. He just acts like one at twenty-four. Maybe he does it because that's just who he is. Maybe he does it because his body really does feel old. Jay is a big guy—linebacker big—but he's not athletic. He doesn't move around much. At work, he spends most of his time sitting behind the counter at the landfill punching numbers into the calculator and keeping track of the scales at the entrance. At home, he fiddles with the free junk he brings home.

"The workers—they used these claws to take the poles off the trucks. Big, huge claws—with nails." Jay digs his hand down into the sand to demonstrate. "I'm going to see if Mom can help me get a job with the power company today." Jay reaches for his pack and works past the broken zipper to get inside. I chuckle at his energy. Not his physical energy, but whatever energy he gets from somewhere else. The guy is extremely passionate, to the point of obsessive. He'll be stuck on this big-truck-power-line thing for days and, yeah, he'll totally hound Mom until she calls the power company.

"I guess it would be cool to be around those big trucks all day," I encourage with a grin, "but the landfill has big trucks, too. The Hill Climbers, remember?"

"The Hill Climbers aren't as cool as these trucks. They don't have big claws. They just have big tires."

"Big tires are just as cool as claws. Bill will miss you at the landfill if you leave. He says you're the best worker he's ever had, and what about all that free stuff that he lets you keep? You won't get to bring home any cool junk if you work for the power company."

"Mom made cookies." Jay stuffs one in his mouth, totally oblivious to the fact that he dropped our conversation. It doesn't bother me that he doesn't know how it's supposed to work—the "I-say-something-first-then-you-say-something next" stuff—but it sure does bother the snot out of other people. Jay doesn't have any friends. None besides Bill and me—and well, of course Mom, Dad, and Uncle Jon. I guess we all just accepted the fact that this is the way that he holds a conversation. We chalk it up as a "Jay thing."

An Autism thing. We all got used to it. No one else around here is willing to, I guess.

"She made cookies again? Didn't she just make some yesterday?" I ask. I hope he brought extra. I didn't eat lunch. My stomach was in knots over this beach—over Migizi.

"Wait. Is it Saturday? I wonder if the power company is closed." My brother mumbles his thought through cookie pieces. He offers to share the rest of his cookies the no-contact way by placing the baggie in between us.

Mom never has been much of a baker. She's had this 2000 *Best Cookie Recipes* book in a stack with other cookbooks on the back of our kitchen counter for as long as I can remember, but for the past five months she's been baking out of it at least three days a week. She blogs about it from our library's computer. Her last post was about peanut butter cookies and how worry was sticky like peanut butter. That was cookie number forty-eight.

"What kind is it?"

Jay hums an "I-don't-know" and struggles down a swallow so he can stuff a second cookie in. It must be good. He's hardly chewing. I can't tell by looking at him, but I sure can hear it. He leans over his pack with wet smacks and clanks junk pieces onto his lap.

I work cookie number forty-nine out of the bag and bite into it. It's good. It tastes buttery—flaky—almost like a snicker-doodle but without the cinnamon. A sugar cookie. Not bad for a plain cookie. My favorite is number twenty-four—Mocha Java Crunch. Now, that one was as close to perfection as you can get.

"You're not wearing your glasses," Jay says after a dry gulp.

"They're dumb. They don't work," I say and cough to scratch a tickle the crumbs had made. I'd love a glass of milk, but I doubt Jay has a gallon of that in his pack.

"They don't work because they *are* dumb. They don't have a brain, silly kid. Besides, they only have two lenses. I think a good pair of glasses should have more than that."

"Maybe." I stretch my fingers in the sand and work them forward and back until they're buried. Leave it to Jay to be totally literal. I know my glasses don't have a brain, for crying-out-loud. Sheesh. He doesn't get it. No one who doesn't have to wear glasses gets it. I'm not wearing my dumb glasses anymore because *they— don't—work*. My doctor said that this is it. That this last pair is the best that he can do. He said it was up to me if I wanted to wear them or not. Sometimes, they seem like they kind of do a little something, but most times I don't see much difference. Today, I just didn't see the point of messing around with them.

Clickety-clack. Clickety-clack.

Jay is fiddling with the junk pieces on his lap. I've missed that sound. I close my eyes to savor the sleepy sensation I get whenever I hear this noise from him. I asked Mom years ago what she thought the feeling was—was I sick? Was I dying? Was it *cancer*? Grandpa had Hodgkin's Lymphoma. After I learned what those words meant, I swore I had it with every cold that I got. Mom told me cancer didn't work that way, and that the warmth that crawled onto my shoulders and over my head was a good thing—not a bad thing. She said it was happiness from pride and she feels it a lot when she thinks about me and Jay.

"Ten." My *needonnisug* says over the *clickety-clack*. "That would be a better number."

"A better number? For what—lenses?" I say while I watch the orange, shadow-shapes shift and flex in the black behind my lids.

"Yeah. Five on each side. Ten."

"Sure, I guess. The more lenses you have, the greater your chances are to see. Makes sense." I lay back on the beach and use my laced hands as a pillow. Jay's pack would work better, but Jay would never part from his pack to let me use it. I dig the backs of my shoes in the sand until it can support my knees. I yawn.

Clickety-clack. Clickety-clack.

Man, I've missed that sound.

Ten lenses. I know where my *needonnisug* got the idea from. Jay has been sitting in on our practice sessions. Dad and Uncle Jon are teaching me a new song—The Last of the Eagle Talkers. The song is about one of our ancestors. According to legend, this girl had eyes like me—or I have eyes like her—whichever way it goes. The song says Native braves seeking her father's favor would gift him spectacles in hopes of curing his daughter's eyes. I guess one set wasn't enough. The story says the Last Eagle Talker's father made her a special pair of glasses from the gifted lenses.

I haven't learned the whole song, yet, so I don't know if the glasses worked for her or not. It's funny. Not tickle-your-insides-raw-with-laughter kind of funny but weird, stupid, it's-not-fair kind of funny. I have this girl's stupid eyes; Jay has her father's super-cool hands. Mom says that I need to practice choosing joy. I guess I should remember that I'm a lot like the Last Eagle Talker in another way, too. I can talk to eagles just like she could. Why is it so easy to focus on the bad things? It makes it so hard to see any of the good.

"And where would I get glasses like that? With ten lenses? Outside of building a time machine and going back in history to steal them away from our ancestor, Whoever-He-Is," I say.

Seriously, a time machine would be a complete waste of time. I wouldn't know where to go. Gaining legend status is awesome, but our people never wrote anything down. The oldest of our stories were all spread by mouth. Important details got lost in translation—major details—like the who and the when. If I don't get a story sung about me someday, that's okay. No one will know it was me, anyway. The tradition is set to continue for another generation. My dad doesn't have any of the new songs he wants to teach me written down yet either.

Clickety-clack. Clickety-clack.

"Here you go." Jay punctuates the end of his sentence by dropping weight onto the top of my chest.

I sit up and squint against the bright and catch something in my hands. I hold it up and twirl it around in my fingers. The "something" hits into my nose. I would never do this in front of anyone else. Having to examine things this close to my face is just plain embarrassing. I must look like an old man of eighty. The object seems to be glasses. Weird ones with *one, two, three, four, five*—my lips move with the count as my fingers discover movement—*six, seven, eight, nine, ten*. There are ten lenses—five on each side—just like the pair from the song.

"You built a time machine?" I tease. He doesn't answer. My *needonnisug* doesn't get the whole teasing thing, but that doesn't ever stop me from trying to have fun with him. "Where did you get these?"

"I made you a proper pair of glasses—just like the pair from the song Dad is teaching you." Jay's fingers crinkle through the baggie until he pulls out a cookie. "Bill helped me weld the arms on. Everything else is me. Happy birthday, kid."

My birthday was three months ago. He missed it. I thought he forgot. Jay isn't an emotional, touchy-feely, remember-your-birthday, type of guy. I didn't really think a thing of it. Really, I didn't. It wasn't a good day for me, anyway, so it wasn't a big deal. There hasn't been a whole lot of good days for me in quite a while.

"Wow. You made these?"

They're bulky. Heavy. There's a lot to them. They look and feel kind of like diving goggles without the plastic strap for your head. I slip the glasses stems over my ears and adjust them on the bridge of my nose. Wow, again. I can't see a thing. I didn't think my eyes could see the world any worse.

"Migizi is here. He misses you." Jay moans to his knees and he crawls over until he's in front of me.

"How do you know?" I ask. My cheeks squish into my eyes when I strain to see him. I can't see my brother's features with my squint. I can see two black spots where his eyes should be, but everything else looks smeary and painted on. Things look abstract and kind of not, but mostly like a painting that I saw in a museum on a school field trip of ladies in fancy dresses hanging out on a beach. I remember the painting because, well, it was a painting of a beach. I also remember it because I thought it was dumb that the ladies were dressed up like they were going to church. I guess they could have been having a church service outside. Our church doesn't have air conditioning. In the summer, the auditorium gets stuffy-hot. Church outside wouldn't be a bad idea.

"I know because Migizi's is up there flying around back and forth, back and forth, back and forth..." My brother repeats the direction of Migizi ten times. I know because I counted. That's what I always do to check to see what his number for the day will be. Ten is the number for today. Is it because of my new glasses? Who knows. Maybe.

"Try the first set of lenses. Your eagle looks neat soaring around. His wings are stretched out. Can you see the wind moving through the tips of his wing fingers?"

Wing fingers. Now, that's a new one. I close my eyes to ease the ache from the lenses. I miss seeing the wind ruffle through Migizi's wings. Wing fingers. That's a neat description that I never thought of before.

"Anything?"

I open my eyes to check and shake my head no.

Click. Click.

My *needonnisug* snaps the next two lenses into position.

"His feathers look like chocolate. Like the insides of the pie that Mom made last Sunday. That was the best. Man, I hope she makes that again. What about now? Can you see anything?"

"Naw. Just blue."

There's nothing soaring around in the color above my brother's head. It's disappointing, but I can't help but smile at the thought of Migizi's feathers painted with the chocolate of Mom's pie. It was a good pie. Jay and I ate the whole thing practically by ourselves.

18

Click. Click.

"Try lenses three and four. He's flying low. Right in front of us. Can you see his head? It's so white. It really stands out against the blue sky. His head looks like a marshmallow. A mini marshmallow because he's so far away, not the regular kind that Mom buys for our bonfires."

"Marshmallow and chocolate. Migizi sounds delicious," I tease.

My brother's descriptions sound silly—and if anyone were on this beach listening, they would have a hearty laugh—but I like them. I like food, and they're working. I can see Migizi. It's been so long...

"Well? Anything? Anything at all?"

"Well, kinda. I think." I scrunch my nose and open my mouth to try to see better. I can't see, but—I can.

Click. Click.

"I think Migizi sees a fish. He's low to the water. Check it out, Jer! His claws are out, just like my truck!"

I strain to see past my *needonnisug* in hopes of seeing a little *something* of Migizi's acrobatics. I understand Jay's excitement about the claws on his truck. My Migizi's talons are my favorite parts of him. I remember how his claws would spear into the Whitefish I would throw up in the air for him catch. When he caught them, my whoops would echo past the trees. It was the coolest thing to watch.

Click. Click.

"Lenses six and seven. Can you see his tail? It almost hit the water. It's open like one of those fans that the old ladies at church use when they're hot. His tail feathers just went—*swoosh*." My brother makes the motion with his arm and spray lands on my face.

"Jay—dude—"

It takes work to keep my comment from sounding like a scold. I wipe my sleeve across the wet spots and I blink behind my goggles—my glasses—to concentrate on the spot that he is manically pointing at.

"He's right there, Jer. Right. There. You can't see him yet, can you?"

I can hear the disappointment in his voice. I shrug and teeter my head back and forth in confusion. I can see Migizi, but I can't. I can't see him with my own eyes, but I can see him through my brother's. Does that count? I don't think it will to Jay. My *needonnisug* won't understand.

I can feel myself smiling again, and the glasses smoosh tighter into the bridge of my nose. I can remember back to the time when I could see clear enough to watch Migizi dive for his fish. I'd grade his skill on a scale of one to ten. I'd give him a ten if he could snatch the fish without getting is wings or tail wet. He used to get a lot of tens.

Click. Click.

"These two are the last and all I have left. Look up, Jer. Look at Migizi. He's right here. *Here*. Above our heads. Can you see him—at all?"

I hum my answer because, yeah, I can see Migizi, but not in the way my brother thinks. I don't want to lose sight of him just yet. It's kind of like Mom's pie on Sunday. It was this fancy punctuation mark at the end of dinner. I didn't go back for another bite of chicken and rice after I finished dessert because I wanted to savor the chocolate taste in my mouth. It's the same thing now but with Migizi. I want to keep the visual that I have of him for as long as I can. I can't see a thing through these glasses—not a flim-flamin' thing—but oddly, it's not a let-down at all. Jay helped me see Migizi again in another way.

Wa-wa-wa-wa.

"What's Migizi saying?" Jay asks. I need to stall and give my throat muscles time to ease up. I count to his magic number of ten before answering.

"He says he wants to talk with me," I say. "And that he really missed hearing my voice."

He missed me. I love that he missed me as much as I missed him. I love that he waited for me and that he didn't give up on me and leave me before my *needonnisug* got here.

"Well, go on. Talk to him, then. I have more things I can work on while I wait. Ice cream." Jay adds the random thought naturally.

"Ice cream," I repeat, and I ask for its importance with wide eyes.

"Do you want to get some when you and Migizi are done talking?"

When you and Migizi are done talking. I love my brother. Somehow, he knew I that I needed to see my eagle—and somehow, he figured out the perfect way to get me out here.

"Only if it's Blue Moon," I say. "But you know what Mom will say, '*You two will spoil your dinner.*'" My squeaky impersonation sounded more like our grandma when she had bronchitis.

Jay pauses from his work on a new gadget. "You sound nothing like Mom."

"True, but she's a girl and I'm a guy so—my voice can only go so high." I laugh. Wow. That felt weird, but it felt *really* good. How long has it been since I last laughed?

Clickety-clack. Clickety-clack.

"Do you think I'm weird?" Jay asks without looking up.

The random questions he fits into the oddest of places aren't a shock to me. Not anymore. Not like they used to be when I was little. As I grew, my understanding of him grew, too. I eventually figured out that his brain is in constant motion—kind of like how my legs are. I pump them up and down when I'm forced to sit. So, honestly? Yeah. Jay can be super-weird, and he can irritate the crud out of me, but this is different from how the others feel. They want him to change. They want him to act normal. I love my *needonnisug*. I don't want him to change at all.

"Yeah, sometimes I do," I tell him in truth, but I quickly add, "but you're a good weird. You're so smart, Jay. I wish I were as smart as you."

I really do, too. If I were, I would only need help *seeing* my Algebra, not help *doing* it, too.

"I wish I were you," he says. He stops his clicking to snap his fingers. It's one of the things he does when he's upset.

"No, you don't, buddy. You're super-cool just the way you are. You wouldn't want to be me; I can't see, remember?"

"If I were you, I wouldn't need any help with anything. I could call the power company on my own. I wouldn't need Mom so much." Jay adds rocking back and forth to the rhythm of his fingers.

"I need help all the time," I correct. I use the calm and understanding tone that I have heard Mom, Dad, and Uncle Jon use on him. "Mom and Dad have to help me with my school work every night because I can't see my stuff anymore. The doc had to order me a special computer to magnify things, remember? The UPS guy should be bringing it any day now. See? I need help."

"I don't think you need help. You never ask for it," he says. My big *needonnisug* knows me better than I thought. He's right. I don't ever ask for help. I'll struggle and squint and try to do as much on my own as possible, even if it means taking twice as long to finish. "If you need help all the time, then name something else," he says. "That was just one thing." His slows his finger snapping down so he can hear my response.

"Well, running. I haven't run in like— forever. There. *Two* things," I confess and hammer the same number of fingers in the wind.

"Could I help you with that? Since my glasses didn't work?"

"I don't know. Maybe," I stammer. This is new. He's never asked to help me with anything before. I guess I could use his help to run again, but can I do it? *Can* I accept it?

22

"Do you think helping is bad or something? Is that why you don't know?" Jay asks. His snapping has become exceptionally loud. How is it louder than the moving water in front of us? "If you do, you shouldn't. Mom says our mission here should be serving one another. That's the same as helping, Jer. My job as your big brother is to tell you when you're wrong. You're wrong, kid."

Wow. Since when have our roles been reversed? I'm usually the one looking out for him. My *needonnisug* does have a point. I must think help is bad, because I turn my back on it any chance I get. I don't mind helping Jay. As a matter-of-fact, I like it. It makes me feel good to help him. Maybe I'm keeping others from feeling the same awesome feeling when I refuse them. Mom says to choose joy in all things. Maybe the key to finding joy is all about how I look at it. Maybe I shouldn't think of myself as a weak failure if I need help—I don't think Jay is—and when I accept it, I shouldn't think that all my independence is forever lost. Jay is impressively independent, and he's autistic. Why must I feel like I'm on the losing end when someone asks to help? Help could mean gain, especially if my *needonnisug* is giving it. I could spend time with my brother again. Isn't that part of what I've been missing?

I can't believe I'm doing this.

"I'd love your help with running," I say as I exhale.

Wow. That didn't feel as bad as I thought it would.

"We can start with a half-mile. Monday morning, before school and work. How does that sound?" I ask, even though I know Jay won't remember when Monday rolls around. I'll have to remind him before bed and in the morning, right before we go.

Is this real? Do I really feel a little less angry? I think *this* is what Mom meant when she said to choose joy. I think I was expecting some joy-to-the-world-the-Lord-is-come, angel-choir moment. Maybe it's like that for some people, but maybe it doesn't have to be just the one way. I wonder if joy can't be subtle and sweet most days. Like the taste of Mom's chocolate pie.

"Dad knows about you, you know—that you can talk to eagles. He told me what your Native name is. You'll love it. It's pretty cool." Jay stops his rocking to fiddle with the zipper on his jacket.

"It's not *Gagiibiingwe Apakwaanaajiinh* by any chance, is it?" I ask. I'm totally serious and not even joking, but this cracks him up.

"No!" My brother falls back into the sand with a snort. It's the silly noise that he makes in place of a laugh. He raises his hands. I can see enough to tell that he's shaking them, like the dancing birch leaves rustling behind us. It's what he does with his hands when he's happy. Really happy. "It's Eagle Eyes, silly kid. I don't know why Dad chose it, though. It would have fit if the glasses worked, but they didn't. I know you couldn't see a thing with them. You didn't answer me when I asked. I know it's because you didn't want to hurt my feelings."

"You tried, though. You did a great job, *needonnisug*," I apologize. I don't hug into him or pat his back to comfort him. He wouldn't like that. I hold my closed fist up to touch him the only way my *needonnisug* will tolerate. Our knuckles bump and the warmth that scared me years ago, creeps across my shoulders and spreads to the top of my head.

My brother is wrong. My new name *will* fit. I think I can see. Not with my eyes, of course, but another way. It's been awhile since I've seen my brother. He's different, but that's okay. It seems unfair that anyone should have to struggle with Autism, and it stinks just the same that I have to be blind—but this is how God made us to be. I think I can see that maybe God did this in hopes of making us better—not physically better but stronger, if that makes any sense. Maybe it's not a punishment, but a way to build strength, to build muscle. There are some neat things that have come from our handicaps. Jay can create some awesome things. Would he still know how if he didn't have Autism? I can talk to eagles. Would I still be able to if I could see? I don't know for sure, but I'd guess no. I've never thought about it that way before. I'm different. Being made this way, I know how to help Jay. Jay's

24

different. In turn, he knows how to help me. I don't think we would know how to help each other if we were both born perfect. God seems to think we can handle how he made us, so if He thinks we can handle Autism and blindness, then I think we can, too.

"Hey, Jay?" I ask.

"Yeah?" my brother answers and stuffs his pack under his head.

"Thanks for the glasses."

Jay shakes his hands in the air to reply. "I think I'll have Mom call the power company on Monday. Today is Saturday. I don't think the power company is open on Saturdays."

Wa-wa-wa-wa.

The sound came from the sky.

I press a handful of sand to my castle. I'm not good at making castles. I don't usually make them when I come out to the beach. I come here to talk to Migizi. I push my new glasses higher to the bridge of my nose. I can't see a thing out of them, but they sure are cool. They helped me to see.

"Migizi," I shout up to the sky. "I'm ready when you are."

Wa-wa-wa-wa.

Migizi is always ready.

SNEAK PEEK FOR *LETTERS FROM THE DRAGON'S SON*

Husbands don't usually get the opportunity to watch their wives grow up. I got to. She's my girl.

I was just a boy when the chief gave her to me. He said she was to be mine until it was safe for her to come home again. I accepted this calling from him without question, though at the time it was out of duty and as penance to pay for the horrible things that the captain and I did—to his land . . . to his people . . .

Izzy's water broke a full day ago. The burn that has been smoldering in my fingertips since her labor began has now spread to the sticky creases of my elbows. The captain. Why must I think of him now?

Izzy whimpers, and I lean forward and take hold of her hands. I press them between my palms and rock like the nervous, expectant father that I am. I kiss into them before stretching out my fingers to relax them. I hope it wasn't my hold on her belly that caused the noise. I don't think it was, she's been struggling like this for hours, but just in case, I whisper an apology into our hands. I need to offer her more. What do other husbands say in times like this? I close my eyes and fill my nose with a long draw of air. I hold it and rest my cheek on our laced hands to give my brain time to find the right words. Encouragement used to come so easily—so instinctively. I've never had to stall before. In the past, the right words would always just . . . come.

"Soon, my love. Soon," I say as I exhale.

That's it? That was terrible. I'm not a comforter, I'm a fortune-telling, grim reaper. I did nothing but announce the devastating loss to come. I need to be here for her—completely here, but he's tugging—tugging—forever the man is tugging. I squeeze my eyes shut until my mouth and nose scrunch together like a ball of paper. I used to do this as a boy to keep him out. It didn't work then. It's not working now.

The captain. I used to call him father—but that was before. Never again will I call him that. I lost my father before the Great War, before he discovered the profits to be found here, and before the death of my mother. It was the ocean's call that stole him from me. It was the trips to the Orient that changed him. Lost. You lose coins or pins, not people. I haven't seen him since the Natives dragged him off. Lost. Dead. It doesn't matter. It's no different to me than the threepenny bit that fell out of my pocket while I was gardening yesterday. I didn't go back to look for it. I knew I wouldn't find it. My father is gone to me just the same.

I did it without him. It seems impossible that a child could raise another—but it happened. Fortunately for Izzy, Miss Margaret helped me. Head house keeper and mother, I couldn't have done it without her. The three of us made an odd little family. Miss Margaret took it upon herself to teach her the things that I could never know. Girl things like dresses, tea, and sewing. I taught Izzy the important things like how to balance a spoon on one's nose and how to slide down a banister.

Izzy. She's the one positive thing that's come from the captain. If we didn't come here and do what we did, I wouldn't have her. I shouldn't think too hard on that. It sounds wrong. It feels wrong. My hands are numb. He's in my head. I know what is to come if I can't get him out.

Izzy and I have only been married for a few short seasons, but I know her as one would when married a lifetime. I know each cry and what makes it better. I know what words she wishes to speak when none can be found. Izzy has been woven into me. The love that I developed for her was painful, for I never expected her to ever love me in return—and now, our baby is coming. At this moment, I couldn't love my sweet girl more. She's brave. She's every bit the princess of our legend.

"Waabishkaa Ma'iingan," she chokes.

Her face is scrunching the cute way it does right before she cries. She doesn't hide her face with cupped hands or buried in my chest like she used to do. Now, she shares her pain with me, and it melts my heart just as it did when I was a boy. I can't answer her call to me. I'll sound weak to her, and she needs my strength. I can only stroke back her hair to acknowledge I know why she calls me that. She wants me to help her just as I did at the fire.

Was my father with my mother when I was born? Mikonan told me that it's not customary for English husbands to be with their wives during childbirth—so maybe he wasn't. I don't have anyone to ask. Like Father, Mother is dead. She's buried under a thorny blanket of roses. My father isn't in the ground next to her where he should be—he's entombed in dragon's flesh instead.

Another wave of pain washes over Izzy, and she curls in a ball towards me. She moans into the bedcoverings and stops her noise when the pain reaches its peak. She's been doing this since early afternoon. It's now evening. Instead of pushing with the urge as her brother instructs her to do, she sucks in a deep breath to fight against it. Her episodes are now minutes apart. Mikonan says it shouldn't be long—but he doesn't know his sister the way I do.

"Brother, tell her she must." Mikonan is at the foot of the bed. He leaves crimson prints on the bed coverings when he adjusts her to her back.

She's doing what any mother would do. She's trying to protect her child. It's what her own mother had done for her. I can't lose both of them. The threatening thought is fueling the tremors that I can feel just beneath my skin. I begin a battle of my own to keep it hidden.

"Niinimooshe, please," I say. When the pain passes, I pull her up and work myself behind her to let her lean on me. I gather her hair and comb away the clinging pieces with my fingers. Another wave is coming. I can tell because she's filling her fists with bedding. Air hisses past her clenched teeth, and her body swells against my chest. She empties her lungs, but it's not to do the work that she must do.

"Nimaamaa," she cries.

She called out for her mother. The mother who rests in the cemetery on the edge of the woods—the mother who didn't need time in her spirit house to turn to dust.

Mikonan's nod is the signal that it's time to encourage Izzy to try again.

"I know," I say into her neck. I bury my face in the damp, dark folds of her shoulder against the image of her mother that will be forever burned in my memory. The hand tremors want to come but I can't let them.

Mikonan notices. My hands are over hers on her stomach and they aren't as still as I thought they were. His brows angle. He knows I haven't been taking the powder.

Izzy is stubborn and even with all the coaxing from me, she refuses to cooperate. The stain on the bed is growing—and the color deepening. This infuriates Mikonan.

"Biis Nigig, if you do not do this now, you will leave Waabishkaa Ma'iingan alone and break your promise. Do you remember?"

A sob bubbles from her throat, and she nods. His words had stolen her back from her mother. She covers my hands with hers the same way she did to seal our marriage vow. Her hands are a salve to my tremors but her touch, as of late, has been losing its potency. I know my unsteady hands are merely hushed quiet. My tremors are patient. They always come back.

This time when Mikonan asks her to push, she obeys. He exhales in relief and I get a look that I haven't seen in a while.

My brother-in-law doesn't say much about how I raised her. He and Odedeyan are grateful and are careful to keep their observations to themselves—but I know what he's thinking. He's thinking that he could have done better. I can see it on his face and I can see it in his posture on the days like today when Izzy ignores all common sense. I don't blame him. I don't know why Odedeyan trusted a messed-up, fifteen-year old to care for his only daughter. It's an insane thought and nearly twelve years later, I still marvel at his decision.

Mikonan has told me before that he had always felt as if he were Izzy's first guardian. He was only seven when he appointed himself to the position when Izzy was born. If Odedeyan would have appointed him instead, and if he were to have fled to England to hide her, the man wouldn't have done any better than me—we are the same age. Then again, maybe he would have done better. My native brother isn't the monster that I am.

My brother-in-law is disappointed. His Biis Nigig didn't outgrow her spirited tongue and stubborn attitude. I know he thinks that I spoiled his Little Otter—but he wasn't there. He didn't have to hear her daily screams and cries when her bandages were changed. He didn't see the raw bubbled skin beneath them. I did. I spoiled her because I felt she had enough sorrow for a lifetime. I love my brother-in-law, but sometimes—I don't think he has a clue as to what he missed those twelve years while we were away.

It only takes a few strains. The ease of the birth makes me wonder how much shorter Izzy's suffering could have been. Mikonan hunches over the baby. I watch his shoulders shift as his hands work. Izzy swallows. She must be watching, too. I reach for the cup of water on the table next to us. I help her drink from it but close my eyes to shut out my brother. In the dark, Izzy's gulps replace that of celebration, her exhausted exhale—our infant's cry.

The cabin is an empty package at Christmas.

I should have listened to Izzy at the dock in England. I never should have brought her back. The soil here is soaked in blood and packed with flesh, yet the earth of the New World desires more. I deserve to be here—to be a forever caretaker to the land that I had bruised with the captain—but not my girl—not my child.

Binidee has slipped in, and she is at the table making the needed preparations. She's ready by her husband's side by the time the baby is ready to be handed off. I wish she had worn her English shoes. Moccasins are silent on these floors. Hard soles would at least fill the room with something. The cabin's silence is a wad of cotton to my ears.

Binidee makes swift work with the baby's bath, and she pats it dry before bundling it snug. She takes a moment to admire it before placing it gently in a waiting basket lined with rabbit fur.

Mikonan rises and wipes his hands on his way over to his wife. He slips an arm around her waist to get a look at the baby. They've been married for only a few short weeks, but they look like two halves that have always been a whole. Their marriage was arranged by Odedeyan, but all of us know it was done by Izzy's influence. My wife did well to persuade her father. They complement each other; in their handsome physical attributes and the way they work together with a seamless ease. Mikonan leans in and whispers instructions before going over to the shelf where I tucked away the Valerian root. My grip on Izzy's hands are twofold. For her and for me. He's going to force me to take it. I can only imagine what the root must taste like, it smells rancid, but that's not the problem. I hid it behind the coffee because I don't want his medicine. I don't want any medicine.

Binidee makes quick work of reversing the damage to Izzy and to the bed. When I try to move, she shakes her head and motions for me to stay. Once things are back in order, she sits at the edge of the bed and asks if we are ready to meet the baby. I nod for the both of us. Izzy is too preoccupied with keeping her tears back; I can feel her gasps against my chest. She's successful—until the basket comes. The sight of it unravels her and her sobs threaten to undo her brother as well. He's just crushed his thumb instead of the Valerian root.

Izzy doesn't reach for the baby when Binidee offers her to her. Her hands are clenched tight on her lap, and she hides them and herself deeper under my arms. I offer my sister-in-law one of mine, for that is all that is needed to accept the little cocoon of leather. I open the leather piece and a sigh escapes. The baby is perfect, and a sob of my own pierces my throat when I see it's a little girl. Tiny fingers, with delicate nails curve over my finger when I lift her hand.

"Look, niinimooshe. Isn't she pretty?" My voice flees from the question that I had used to describe our baby. Izzy heard and understood my constricted whisper, and she nods in agreement. She's still tight against me and won't reach for her.

She's a woman of nineteen years, yet sometimes, I still see glimpses of the little girl that I used to know. Right now, she is the timid child that was afraid of the grass beneath her feet when I brought her outside to the gardens for the first time.

I know regret and I know it's a burden that I don't want my wife to carry. I take her hand and guide one of her fingers over the baby's head and continue the journey down to her neck and to her rounded tummy.

"She's the color of your mother's roses," Izzy finally rasps, "glossed with dew. She's beautiful."

My wife's description was kinder than what mine would have been. She is precious and beautiful, but she also wasn't ready to be born. The longer I admire her, the clearer the pictures become of Izzy. Her mother. Her grandfather. Faces of others that I never got to know but saw in the village. My perfect daughter has been licked pink by the same dragon's flame. Exhaustion gives my throat permission to open, and I sob into Izzy's hair. The baby's death is my fault.

I give up reigning in my hand tremors and let my muscles have their way.

Mikonan steps forward with a steaming cup of the powdered, rotten root, but Binidee stops him. I'm glad that she did. It's getting harder to say no. The medicine will bring relief, but I don't want any strange powders. I don't want to be like *him* in that way. I don't want what little there is left of me to die.

"No. He needs to mourn. He will never deal with the sorrow properly if you send him off to sleep." Binidee then nods down to Izzy. "Pain is a powerful teacher. Let them find each other."

Izzy gathers the baby from my hand and cuddles her to her chest. Even though her eyes are glossy and bagged, they are still beautiful in their exhausted state. Tears have made the golden amber shine like honey within the brown hues. In the darkest of them, crimson flecks are hidden that crackle with spirit when she's angry.

A soft, dove-like moan is all she can muster as she turns to snuggle back under my arm. This sound is new. I don't know what to do or what will work to ease it. This causes my muscles further distress. Her free hand clamps over mine and its strength wrestles my hand until it's still. I whisper an apology to her. I will never be finished asking my wife for forgiveness. She doesn't know the things he made me do. The baby is yet another aftershock of the damage that the Dragon has cultivated.

The captain is here, and I don't know how to rid myself of him.

A Glimpse of the Upper Peninsula

AUTHOR'S NOTE

I can't remember a time without glasses.

I got my first pair when I was in fourth grade. I remember my mom and a lady in a white coat holding out frames and asking which one I liked the best. Strangers made me nervous. I'm sure I had one of my stomach aches and was too afraid to share my opinion beyond a nod or a point. Over the years it's gotten easier for me to choose a pair of frames. I discovered it's possible to use my voice *and* have a stomach ache at the same time—and it helps that I don't have to move beyond the beefy, plastic section. My options have shrunk with my ever-thickening lenses.

White Wolf and the Ash Princess did quite the number on my weak eyes. There's a lot of computer work that comes with publishing a book. Within the past year, I have seen both my ophthalmologist and optometrist more times than I care to count. Double vision, smeared vison, tired eyes, and migraine headaches are side effects from spending hours on the laptop. That's my diagnosis, anyway. The three different doctors I saw didn't say much when I asked them what was going on. They just prescribed lenses, shrugged, and shoved me off to the lady in the white coat to get my bill.

What the doctors *do* know is that I'm not going blind. They told me that only because I asked. I'm pretty sure I asked the question at every appointment since that first visit when I was ten. That still doesn't quench my fear. I saw what happened to Mary on *Little House on the Prairie*. Remember that two-part episode when Mary's pretty blue eyes go dark? Yeah, unfortunately, I can't forget about it either.

Changes. How do we deal with them? To find out, I wrote *Eagle Eyes.* I saw the solution wasn't a suggestion. It was a command.

Rejoice always, pray continually, give thanks in all circumstances; for this is God's will for you in Christ Jesus." I *Thessalonians 5: 16-18*

I've been practicing and failing at this for months. God knows how difficult it is. That's why He repeats this in Philippians 4:4 to encourage us to try and try again:

"Rejoice in the Lord always. I will say it again: Rejoice."

Finding joy in difficult circumstances is never easy to do. Jeremy discovered that it takes practice. Sometimes, it takes years. Oftentimes, it's a lifetime struggle. Don't give up when you fail. Keep up the fight.

Practice joy with me, dear reader. Remember we are a people with *hope.* Romans 10:13 reassures us that EVERYONE who calls on the name of the Lord will be saved. We can rejoice in that fact alone that we WILL be free from our fragile bodies someday. The lame will be made to walk again, and the blind will see. Our bodies will be perfect in the way that He intended before sin.

I'm dreading my next eye appointment. I know what's going to happen. After my exam, the lady in the white coat will lead me to the "chubby" section. I'll be tempted to moan an internal *why* when I walk out of the clinic with a heavier of set of glasses on my nose. I'll have to put to practice the verses He wants me to remember. I will not despair. I will not fret. I'll rejoice because He has a new pair of eyes waiting for me in heaven.

Tammy Lash

A Special Thank You

Rebeka Borshevsky, Annie Pavese, Kelsey Lash, Austin Lash, Ryan Lash: Thank you for your support, suggestions, feedback, and proofing. Thank you for your encouragement and gentle nudges to continue writing myself into the world of White Wolf. I love you all so very much!

Savannah Jezowski, my best friend, editor, interior formatter, and designer: You are my anchor in the writing industry. Thank you for yanking me up out of the muddy waters of self-doubt and encouraging me forward. You give me the courage to explore my dark places so I can map a way out for others. I love you, sister.

Mom: Thank you for letting me cry when things are tough. Thank you for reminding me to keep the faith, to trust God in all things, and for the phrase "Everything will work out in the right way at the right time," right when I needed it. I love you more than words can say.

Kris: Thank you for being the godly role model that you are so I can infuse you into my male characters. I don't feel guilty spending time with them—they are you, after all. You are forever etched in my heart. I love you.

Jesus: Thank you for letting me struggle with each word that I type. It is a reminder that I can't do this work on my own. My stories are Yours. Thank you for Your patience and faithfulness. When I am weak, You are strong. (II Corinthians 12:10)

ABOUT THE AUTHOR

Tammy lives in Michigan's Upper Peninsula near the shores of Lake Superior with her husband and three teen/adult children. Currently, they are working together on their "new" home just outside the Hiawatha National Forest she writes about in her stories.

Tammy enjoys hiking, kayaking, beach wandering, "hunting" for birch bark, and spotting migizis.

She is the author of *White Wolf and the Ash Princess*, the coming sequel, *Letters from the Dragon's Son*, and the short story *Eagle Eyes* from the Descendants of White Wolf series.

CONNECT WITH TAMMY

Website@tammylash.wordpress.com
Facebook@tammylashauthor
Twitter@TammyLash5
Instagram@tamlash5
Pinterest@tamlash5
Goodreads@Tammy_Lash

ALSO AVAILABLE FROM TAMMY LASH

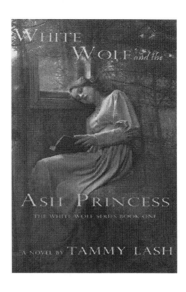

Eighteen-year-old Izzy's limited world begins to feel cramped after she completes her self-appointed book dare. After reading two-hundred and fifty books, a thought that had been once tucked away as tightly as the books on her library shelves becomes too irresistible to ignore . . . "Who am I?"

Memory loss prohibits Izzy from remembering her life before age seven when she was injured in a fire. Jonathan Gudwyne and his head housekeeper rescued her and took Izzy in as their own, but who did she belong to before they took her in?

Crippling panic keeps Izzy from wandering beyond the stables but Tubs, the Gudwyne's young stable boy, encourages Izzy to go beyond the property's rock wall to a world that promises possible answers, but also great danger. A scorched castle in the woods and a mysterious cellar filled with secrets sets Izzy on a path to the New World, where she will not only have to face her own terror but face the people responsible for her scars.

It is here, in the untamed wilds of the seventeenth century that she finds love and a home in the most unexpected of places.

AVAILABLE ON AMAZON

Made in the USA
Columbia, SC
01 September 2022

66461560R00037